My Shadow and I

by Patty Wolcott

illustrated by Frank Bozzo

Addison-Wesley

"To all children who are learning to read"

Addisonian Press titles by Patty Wolcott

Beware of a Very Hungry Fox

The Cake Story

The Forest Fire

I'm Going to New York to Visit the Queen

The Marvelous Mud Washing Machine

My Shadow and I

Pickle Pickle Pickle Juice

Super Sam and the Salad Garden

Tunafish Sandwiches

Where Did That Naughty Little Hamster Go?

An Addisonian Press Book

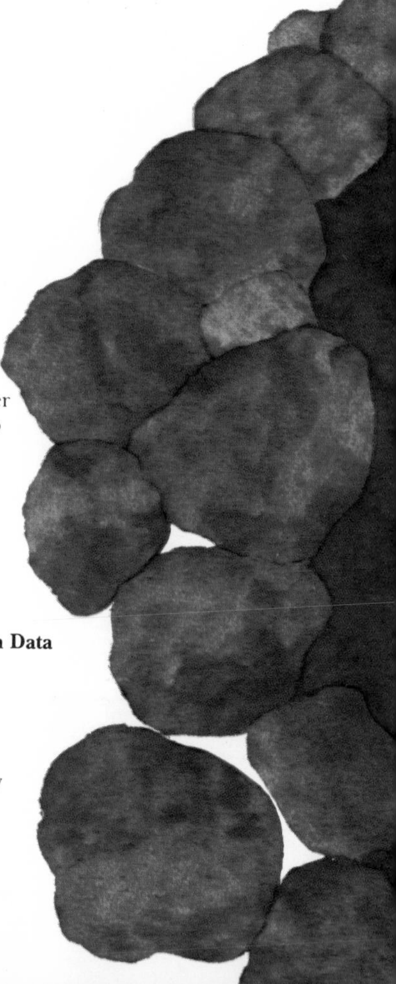

Addison-Wesley Publishing Company, Inc.
Reading, Massachusetts 01867
Printed in the United States of America
First Printing

WZ/WZ 9/75 14251

Library of Congress Cataloging in Publication Data

Wolcott, Patty.
My shadow and I.
SUMMARY: As the large old tree near his house seems to become a frightening monster, a little boy and his shadow battle this adversary with their broom-weapons.
"An Addisonian Press book."
I. Bozzo, Frank, illus. II. Title.
PZ7.W8185My [E] 74-5012
ISBN 0-201-14251-1

My Shadow and I
walk together,
Shadow and I,
Shadow and I.

I walk and walk,
and my Shadow walks,

Shadow and I,
Shadow and I.

My Shadow and I
run together.
Run, Shadow, run!
Run, Shadow, run!

I run and run,
and my Shadow runs,

Shadow and I,
Shadow and I.

My Shadow and I
fight and fight.
Fight, Shadow, fight!
Fight, Shadow, fight!

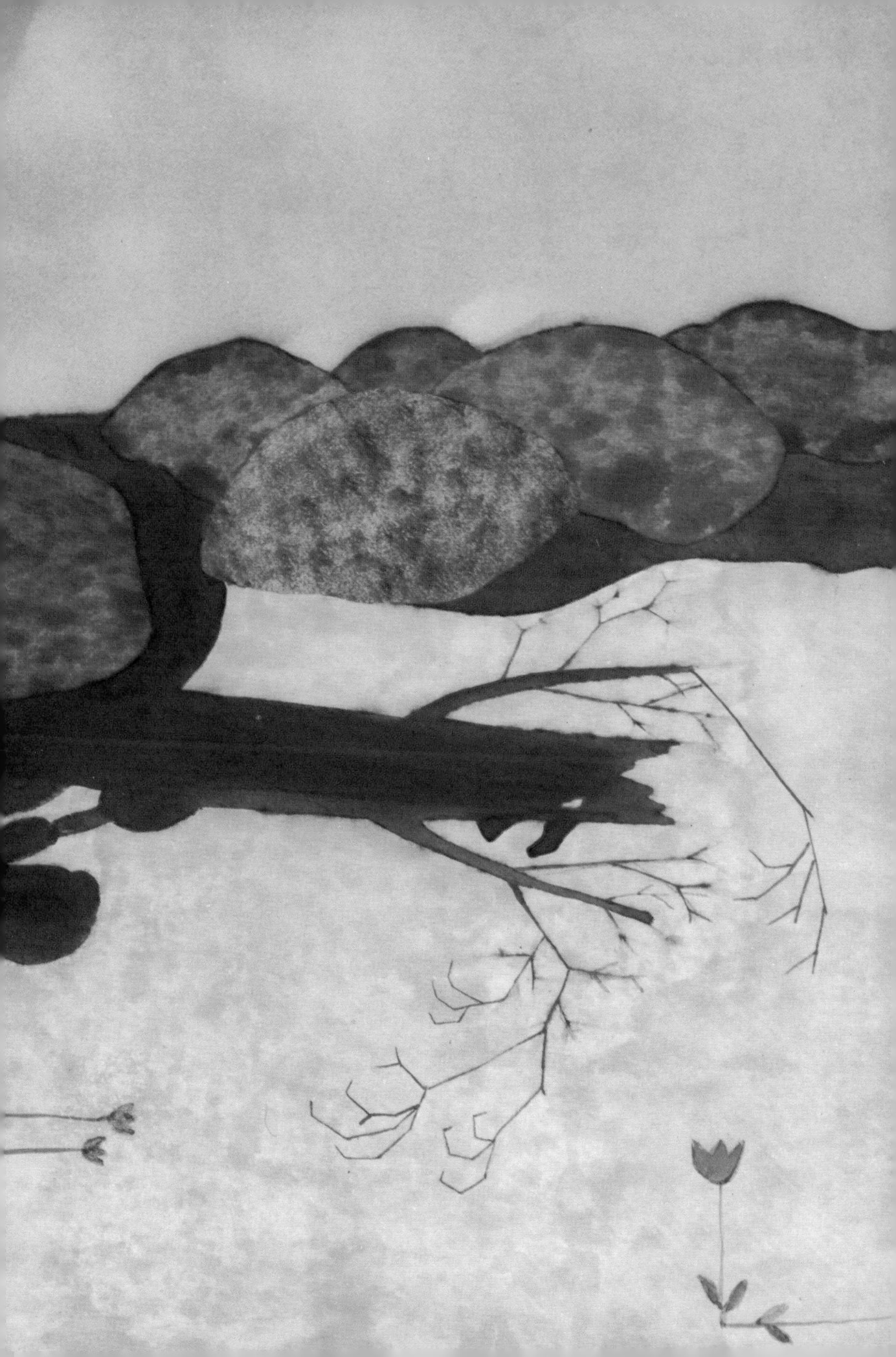

I fight and fight,
and my Shadow fights,

Shadow and I,
Shadow and I.

My Shadow and I
win together,
win together,
Shadow and I.

My Shadow and I
dance together.
Dance, Shadow, dance.

I dance and dance,
and my Shadow dances,
Shadow and I,
Shadow and I.